PEDRO

FIRST-GRADE
HERO

by Fran Manushkin

illustrated by
Tammie Lyon

CAPSTONE PRESS
a capstone imprint

Pedro is published by Picture Window Books,
a Capstone Imprint
1710 Roe Crest Drive
North Mankato, Minnesota 56003
www.mycapstone.com

Text © 2016 Fran Manushkin
Illustrations © 2016 Picture Window Books

Library of Congress Cataloging-in-Publication Data

Names: Manushkin, Fran, author. | Lyon, Tammie, illustrator.
Title: Pedro, first grade hero / Fran Manushkin; [illustrated] by Tammie Lyon.
Description: North Mankato, Minnesota : Capstone Press, [2017] | Series:
    Pedro | Summary: A collection of four separately published stories featuring
    Pedro, Katie Woo's classmate and friend.
Identifiers: LCCN 2016002727 | ISBN 9781515801122 (pbk.)
Subjects: LCSH: Hispanic Americans—Juvenile fiction. | Elementary schools—
    Juvenile fiction. | Friendship—Juvenile fiction. | CYAC: Hispanic
    Americans—Fiction. | Schools—Fiction. | Friendship—Fiction.
Classification: LCC PZ7.M3195 Pb 2017 | DDC 813.54--dc23
LC record available at http://lccn.loc.gov/2016002727

Designers: Aruna Rangarajan and Tracy McCabe

Design Elements: Shutterstock

Photo Credits:
Greg Holch, pg. 96
Tammie Lyon, pg. 96

Printed and bound in the USA.
009901R

Table of Contents

PEDRO GOES
BUGGY

"Who likes bugs?" asked Miss Winkle.

"I do!" yelled Pedro. "I am wild about bugs!"

"Me too," said Katie Woo.

"I like the green bugs that are called katydids."

"Ha!" Pedro smiled. "You would!"

"We are going to study bugs,"
said Miss Winkle. "After school,
go out and look for bugs. Pick one
that you like and write about it."

"I like stinkbugs!" shouted
Roddy. "I can bring one to school.
That would be fun!"

"Not a good
idea," said Miss
Winkle.

Pedro went home and found his
bug jar.

He began looking for bugs in
the weeds. He found ten ants and
put them in his jar.

Pedro told JoJo, "Flies are fun

too. But they are hard to catch."

"Not for my cat," bragged JoJo.

"Spiders are cool," Pedro told
his mother. "I'll bring some home."

"No way!" said his mom. "Ants
are fine, but no spiders."

Pedro found a field with lots of ladybugs. He took home fifteen. His puppy, Peppy, tried to eat them.

"No way!" yelled Pedro.

Pedro loved
beetles too.

"They are so
shiny," he told JoJo.
"And they are fun to
say," he added. "Beetle,
beetle, beetle!"

He took home twenty.

Pedro couldn't stop catching
bugs! Each day he found more.

He told his little brother, Paco,
"It's a good thing I have a big jar!"

One day, when Pedro was in school, Paco told the bugs, "I want to watch you run around."

He opened the jar and let them all out!

There were bugs on the bed and
bugs on Paco's head.

"Cool!" he said.

When Pedro came home, he
said, "Not cool!"

"Out they go!" Pedro's dad said. "These bugs are driving me buggy."

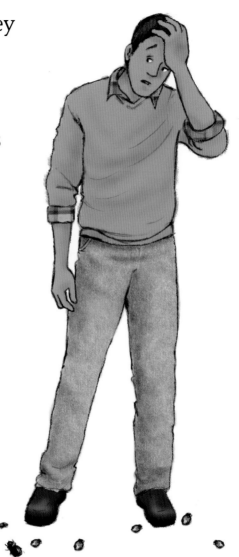

The next day, Pedro told Katie,
"I have no bugs to write about."
"You better hurry and find
one," said Katie. "Get hopping."

"I love hopping!" said Pedro. He hopped down the block, looking for a new bug.

He saw a wasp. "No way!" he yelled.

He saw a grasshopper jumping

in the weeds.

"Let's race!" Pedro said.

Pedro hopped. The grasshopper jumped.

"It's a tie!" said JoJo. "You both win!"

Pedro told the grasshopper,

"You are the most fun. I will write

about you."

Pedro wrote about the
grasshopper. Then he let him go.

"Good work," said Miss Winkle. "Next we will be writing about tigers."

"Great!" Pedro smiled. "I can't wait to bring one home."

PEDRO'S BIG
GOAL

Pedro didn't like soccer. He

LOVED soccer. He loved running

and kicking and jumping.

"Our team is the best!" he
bragged. "Hurray for the Jumping
Wildcats."

Katie Woo cheered too. "We run fast. We jump high. We kick hard!"

Coach Rush said, "Next week, I'm picking a goalie for our first game. Who wants to try out?"

"Me! Me! Me!" yelled everyone.

"Forget it," sneered Roddy.

"I'm the biggest.
Nobody can
beat me."

"Roddy's right," said Pedro. "He will be the best."

"I'm not so sure," said Katie. "Bigger is not always better."

Katie and JoJo and Barry went
home with Pedro to practice.

Katie kicked the ball to Pedro.

WHOOSH! It went past him.

"Try again!" yelled Barry. He
kicked the ball to Pedro.

WHOOSH! Pedro missed again.

Pedro told his dad, "Maybe
I can't move fast enough to be
a goalie."

"Don't give up!" said his dad.

"Okay," agreed
Pedro. "I'll
keep trying."

"I want to play too," said Pedro's brother, Paco.

"Watch out!" Pedro shouted.

He blocked Paco from jumping into a pile of puppy poop.

"Good block!" said Pedro's dad.

He kicked the ball to Pedro.

Pedro almost blocked it.

"Keep trying," said his dad.

"You will get better."

The next day, Pedro's friends
came over to play. Barry kicked
the ball.

Oops! He kicked it too hard,
and the ball flew over the fence.

"Arf!" Pedro's puppy, Peppy, chased the ball. He tried to jump over the fence and into the street.

Pedro jumped high. He blocked
Peppy!

"Wow!" cheered Barry. "That was
the best block of all."

"I'll say!" Pedro smiled, hugging
Peppy tight.

Pedro kept on practicing.

"I wonder who the coach will pick to be goalie?" asked Katie.

"Maybe it will be Roddy," said JoJo.

"Maybe not," said Barry.

Finally, the day came for the tryouts. Katie went first. She missed both balls.

"Better luck next time," said Coach Rush.

Then it was JoJo's turn. She blocked one ball, but she missed the next one.

"Not bad," said Coach Rush. "Let's see who can block both balls."

"It's my turn," said Roddy. "I know I will win."

But Roddy was so busy bragging he missed both balls!

Then it was Pedro's turn. Roddy kicked the first ball.

Pedro blocked it!

Roddy kicked the second ball. Pedro jumped.

He blocked that one too!

"You win!" yelled Coach Rush. "Pedro is our goalie."

"Yay!" cheered Pedro's friends. "We knew you could do it."

"Now I know too," said Pedro. "I get a big kick out of this game."

He smiled all the way home.

PEDRO'S MYSTERY CLUB

"I am starting a mystery club!" Pedro told Katie and JoJo. "We can have our meetings here in my new tree house."

"Cool idea!" said JoJo.

"I'm great at solving mysteries,"
said Katie Woo. "I always know where
Mom hides my birthday presents."

"I have a mystery for you," said Pedro's mom. "I can't find my locket."

"That is a small mystery," said Pedro. "But it's a good start."

Pedro wrote down the clues. "Where did you go today?" he asked his mom.

"I went to the store to get chocolate-chip cookie mix," she said.

"I know what to do," said Pedro.
"We will follow the path you took and
find your locket. It will be hard work.
So when we come back, we will need
those cookies."

Katie told Pedro, "I'm glad the sun is out. The locket will sparkle in the sunlight. That will make it easy to find."

"I see it!" yelled Katie. "Oops. I don't. It's just a dime."

"I found a toy ring," said JoJo. "It fits my hand."

But they didn't find a locket.

They came to a big hill. Katie asked, "Do you think your mom walked up this hill?"

"No way," said Pedro. "But I would like to roll down it. It's fun!"

It was!

"Whoops!" said Pedro. "I lost my notebook."

They climbed back up and found the notebook.

"Solving mysteries is hard
work," said Pedro. "I need a drink."
Luckily, his friend Jane was
selling lemonade.

"I saw your mom an hour ago," said Jane. "She got a drink on her way to the grocery store."

"Was she wearing her locket?" asked Pedro.

"She wasn't," said Jane. "I always like looking at the photos inside. But she wasn't wearing it."

They rushed home. Pedro told his mom, "Jane didn't see you wearing your locket on the way to the store. It is still here!"

"I have another mystery," said Pedro's dad. "I can't find my new phone!"

"Did you roll down a hill?"
asked Pedro.

"No," said his dad.

They looked for his phone. They
looked for the locket. No luck.

Pedro said, "Let's take a break from mystery solving. Let's play soccer!"

Katie kicked the ball, but she kicked it too hard. The ball rolled under a bush.

"I'll get it," yelled Pedro.

As he grabbed the ball, he saw something shiny — his mom's locket!

"Yay, Pedro!" she said. "My locket fell off when I was picking roses."

"Now let's find Dad's phone," said
Pedro. "Let's go to our tree house.
That's a good place to think."

JoJo wondered, "If I were a phone, where would I be?"

Katie said, "I wish that noisy bird would stop chirping. I can't think!"

"That's no bird," said Pedro. "It's Dad's phone! Someone is trying to call him." They followed the sound down to the grass.

Pedro's dad smiled. "I dropped it when I was painting your clubhouse."

Katie Woo smiled too. "If your family keeps losing things, we will always have mysteries to solve."

"Quick!" said Pedro. "Before that happens, let's have a snack before someone loses something else."

The snack was no mystery — it was chocolate chip cookies!

PEDRO FOR PRESIDENT

Pedro told Miss Winkle, "I am running for president of our class."

"So am I!" said Katie Woo.

Miss Winkle asked them,
"What can you do for
our class?"

"I can do
magic tricks,"
said Pedro.

"I can tap
dance," said Katie.

"Those are fun," said Miss Winkle. "But how will you help the class?"

"I don't know," said Katie.

"I'll have to think," said Pedro.

That night, Pedro painted a poster.
His brother, Paco, wanted to help. He
put his messy hands all over it.

"I can fix this," said Pedro. He painted:

VOTE FOR PEDRO!

I WILL GIVE YOU

A HELPING HAND!

"Good work," said his father.

"You are using your head."

The next day,
Miss Winkle said,
"Before we vote
tomorrow, Katie
and Pedro will
each give a
speech. You can tell
us why you should
be president."

"I'm not good at giving speeches," said Pedro.

"I am," bragged Katie Woo.

Pedro tried to write his speech.
Just then, Roddy threw a pencil at the
goldfish bowl. Pedro jumped up and
caught the pencil.

"You saved our fish!" cheered
Barry. "And you found my favorite
pencil."

Pedro tried to write his speech again. But he saw JoJo looking sad.

"What's wrong?" he asked.

"I got a bad grade on my math test," said JoJo.

"Don't worry," said Pedro.
"You can do better
tomorrow. Maybe I
can cheer you up
with a joke."

Pedro asked, "Why is 6 afraid of 7?"

"Why?" asked JoJo.

"Because 7 8 9."

"That's funny," said JoJo. "I feel better."

That night, Pedro asked his dad, "What should I say in my speech tomorrow?"

"Arf!" barked Peppy.

"I can't say that!" Pedro joked.

The next day was the election.

Katie gave a great speech.

Miss Winkle asked Pedro, "Is your
speech ready?"

"Um, no," said Pedro.

Roddy yelled, "I want a boy to win. And I know what we should do."

"What?" asked JoJo.

Roddy said, "There are more boys than girls in this class. So if all the boys vote for Pedro, he will win!"

"That's not fair!" said Pedro.
"You should vote for the best
person — boy or girl."

"That was a wonderful speech," said Miss Winkle.

"I'm voting for Pedro," said Barry.

"Me too!" said JoJo. "Pedro is a team player!"

Pedro asked Katie, "Will we still be friends if I win?"

"For sure!" said Katie. "We will always be friends."

They shook on it.

The class counted the votes. Guess who won?

Pedro!

"I promise to be a terrific president for everyone," said Pedro.

And he was!

JOKE AROUND

★ Which bugs do well in school?
Spelling bees

★ What is a bee's favorite treat?
Bumble gum

★ What do spiders like with their hamburgers?
French flies

★ What kind of music do grasshoppers like?
Hip-hop

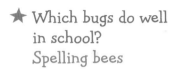

WITH PEDRO!

★ What do you call a soccer player made of swiss cheese?
A holey goalie

★ Why did the soccer ball quit the team?
It was tired of getting kicked around.

★ What did the bumble bee say when it kicked the soccer ball?
"Hived scored!"

★ Why was Cinderella thrown off the soccer team?
She ran away from the ball.

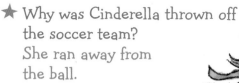

JOKE AROUND

★ What word becomes shorter if you add two letters to it?
Short

★ What has to be broken before you can use it?
An egg

★ What has hands but cannot clap?
A clock

★ What is at the end of a Rainbow?
The letter W

WITH PEDRO!

★ What do librarians take with them
  when they go fishing?
  Bookworms

★ Why did the pony have to stay
  after school?
  For horsing around

★ What happened to make the little
  broom late for school?
  He overswept.

★ Why was the jungle
  animal thrown out
  of school?
  He was a cheetah.

About the Author

Fran Manushkin is the author of many popular picture books, including *Happy in Our Skin*; *Baby, Come Out!*; *Latkes and Applesauce: A Hanukkah Story*; *The Tushy Book*; *The Belly Book*; and *Big Girl Panties*. Fran writes on her beloved Mac computer in New York City, without the help of her two naughty cats, Chaim and Goldy.

About the Illustrator

Tammie Lyon began her love for drawing at a young age while sitting at the kitchen table with her dad. She continued her love of art and eventually attended the Columbus College of Art and Design, where she earned a bachelor's degree in fine art. After a brief career as a professional ballet dancer, she decided to devote herself full-time to illustration. Today she lives with her husband, Lee, in Cincinnati, Ohio. Her dogs, Gus and Dudley, keep her company as she works in her studio.